Copyright © 1986 by Nord-Süd Verlag AG, Gossau Zürich, Switzerland
First published in Switzerland under the title *Die müde Eule*
English translation copyright © 1986 by Jock Curle

First published in the United States, Great Britain, Canada,
Australia, and New Zealand in 1986 by North-South Books,
an imprint of Nord-Süd Verlag AG, Gossau Zürich, Switzerland.
First paperback edition published in 1998 by North-South Books.

Library of Congress Cataloging-in-Publication Data
Pfister, Marcus
The sleepy owl.
I. Title II. Die müde Eule. English
833'.914 [J] P7

A CIP catalogue record for this book is available from The British Library.

ISBN 1-55858-905-8
1 3 5 7 9 PB 10 8 6 4 2
Printed in Belgium

For more information about our books, and the authors and artists
who create them, visit our web site: http://www.northsouth.com

Marcus Pfister

The Sleepy Owl

Translated by J. J. Curle

North-South Books / New York / London

Little Owl lived deep in the woods.
All day long she perched on a branch,
sound asleep.

Each evening, as daylight faded, she woke up.

She did not find getting up easy.
She was a bit of a sleepyhead.

Little Owl yawned and stretched her wings.
"Good evening, everyone," she said. But there
was no one around.
"I wish I had woken up earlier. The other owls
have all gone and I have no one to play with."
Little Owl spread her wings and flew off
into the night sky.

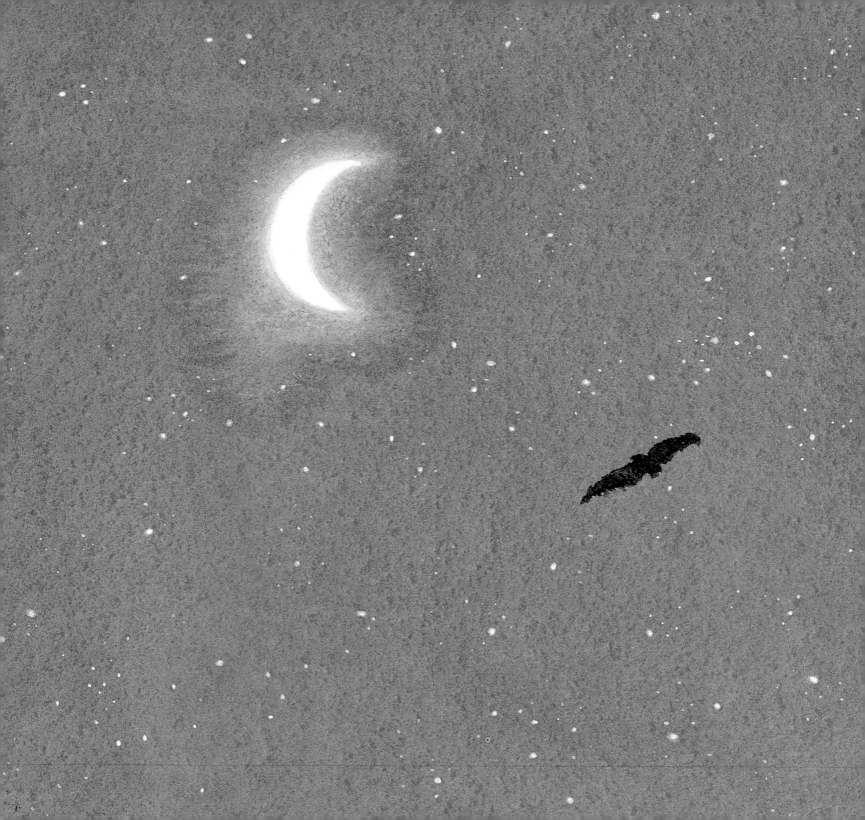

Far below her, Little Owl saw a house.
"I might find a playmate there," she thought.

She swooped down onto a windowsill
and tapped on the glass with her beak.

The sound of the taps woke Tom.

"What do you want?" he said sleepily as he opened the window.

"Come and play with me," said Little Owl.

"I'm much too sleepy. It's the middle of the night! Come back tomorrow afternoon. We can play then."

"How can I wake up in the day?" said Little Owl. "I wake up only at night."

"Take my alarm clock. As soon as you hear it go off, fly straight over here."

Little Owl wondered how the metal contraption could help her. But she picked it up in her claws and flew home.

Back on her branch, Little Owl set the alarm clock down beside her. By now it was day, so she soon fell asleep.

A terrifying noise woke her. It almost made her fall
off her branch. The noisy yellow contraption rang
and shook as though it would never stop.
The noise woke every owl in the woods.
"What's the matter?" they shouted.
"Who's making that horrible noise?"
Owls hate being disturbed in the middle of the day.

Little Owl tried to stretch her wings. But she was too tired and the sunlight hurt her eyes.
Great tears fell down onto her feathers. Her aunt tried to comfort her. "Don't cry," she said. "If you get up in time tonight, you can play with us."

In his home Tom was waiting for Little Owl. What had happened to his new friend? Why hadn't she come?

"Be sensible, Tom," his mother said. "Owls sleep by day, and you sleep at night. So how can the two of you play together? Why not finish painting your kite, instead of moping about."

So Tom got out his paintbox and painted an owl
face on his kite. Then he and his friend Bob played
with it all afternoon.
Now Tom had his own owl to play with, and what's
more, his owl could fly, just like his friend Little Owl.

That evening Little Owl woke up earlier and got up quicker than ever before. She had to take the alarm clock back to Tom. Near his house she found the two boys flying the kite. She saw the picture of herself that Tom had painted on it. How nice!

"Time for bed," Tom's mother called. Tom waved to Little Owl as she flew away.

"He is still my friend, even though we can't play together," thought Little Owl.

And back home in the woods, all the owls were awake and waiting to play with her.